Granny Garbanzo & Snicklefritz

Major Bedhead

THE BIG COMFY COUCH™

Where Are You, Fuzzy?

Written by **Cheryl Wagner**

Illustrated by **Richard Kolding**

TIME LIFE kids

ALEXANDRIA,
VIRGINIA

The Big Comfy Couch is the best place for a clown and her doll to play. And under the Couch is the best place for Dustbunnies to play.

Hide-and-seek used to be Fuzzy Dustbunny's favorite game, because he loved to hide. And Wuzzy Dustbunny was very good at counting to ten. But one day, Fuzzy learned an important lesson about playing.

It all began when he decided to find a *really* good place to hide. Somewhere different. Somewhere fun. Somewhere new . . .

. . . like inside Loonette's dollhouse, where the Foley family lived!

Andy Foley was surprised to have a Dustbunny hiding in his house. Dad Foley didn't notice. He was too busy taking his nap. He didn't hear Wuzzy calling, "Fuzzy! Where are you?"

Wuzzy was upset. Fuzzy was supposed to play hide-and-seek *under* the Big Comfy Couch, not way over there in the Foleys' house. Every Dustbunny knew that. But before Wuzzy could call "One, two, three" on Fuzzy, that mischief-making brother of his ran to the Couch leg.

"Home free!" Fuzzy cried. "You're It!"

So Wuzzy started to count again. And Fuzzy looked for another good place to hide . . .

. . . like on top of the Big Comfy Couch.
Wuzzy would never find him up here!

Fuzzy Dustbunny decided this was the
best game of hide-and-seek he had
ever played in all his Dustbunny
days. Staying under the Couch
all the time wasn't nearly as
much fun.

From way down below, he could hear
a little voice calling, "Fuzzy! Where
are you?"

"Here I am, Wuzzy," Fuzzy called, touching home base. "Home free! You're It again!"

Wuzzy didn't like this game anymore. He was tired of just counting all the time. Anyway, Fuzzy wasn't playing by the rules. Dustbunnies are supposed to play *under* the Big Comfy Couch. Every Dustbunny knew that!

But Fuzzy wasn't even listening. He was having his biggest idea ever . . .

. . . to go where no Dustbunny had ever gone before. Granny Garbanzo's garden! After all, why should Dustbunnies have to stay forever in the same old boring place? Outside would be really exciting!

And it was. Granny's garden was the biggest and best place to play that Fuzzy could imagine. There were new places to climb on, different smells in the air, and tall things to scoot behind. Fuzzy couldn't wait to tell his brother. But before he could call Wuzzy to come out and play . . .

A wild lion tried to
catch him!

A great big claw tried to scratch him!

A monster wheel tried to squish Fuzzy flat!

This garden was *not* a good place at all! It was a scary
place where a Dustbunny could get hurt. Fuzzy wanted to
go home to his brother and the Big Comfy Couch. Now!
But how? He needed help.

"Wuzzy!" he shouted. "Where are you?"

Inside, Wuzzy was busy getting the best help a
Dustbunny can find. That's what doll friends are
for. Every Dustbunny knows that. Could Molly
help bring his brother Fuzzy home where he
belonged, under the Big Comfy Couch, before
something terrible happened?

Just then, Major Bedhead could be heard outside, calling "Special delivery for Loonette the Clown! Special delivery for Loonette!" Loonette skipped out to Granny's garden, and, luckily for a certain Dustbunny, she brought Molly with her.

Granny and Bedhead watched Loonette open her package, while Molly worried about Fuzzy. "Look!" exclaimed Loonette. "It's a fluffy muffler from Auntie Macassar for playing dress-up! Perf!"

Molly knew it would be perfect as something else, too—a fluffy feather taxi! In a whisper so low only Dustbunnies and dolls could hear, she told Fuzzy to hop aboard.

Fuzzy rode home happily to the Big Comfy Couch. He was safe. And he was sorry. He promised Wuzzy and he promised himself he would never again play where Dustbunnies are not supposed to play.

He decided his new favorite game would be Dustbunny tag, which always ends with a big hug for your brother. And the best place for Dustbunny tag in the whole wide world is under the Big Comfy Couch. Every Dustbunny knows that!

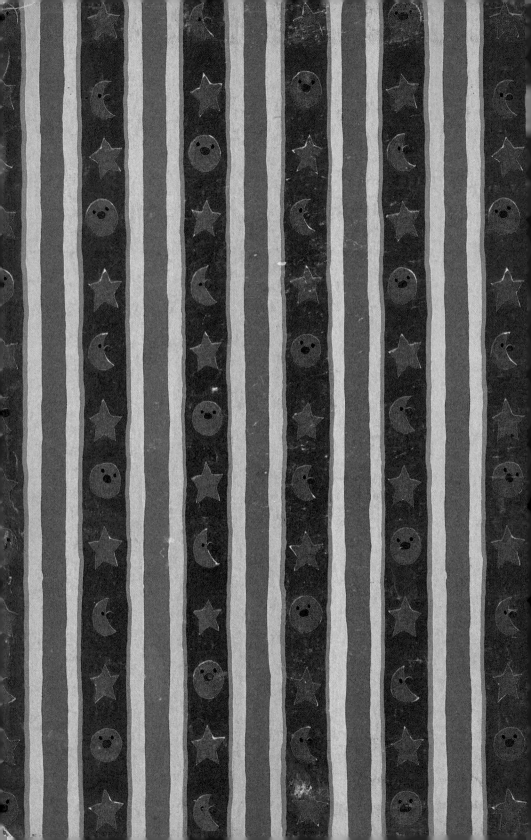